Her Duke to Beguile

Her Duke to Beguile

WAYWARD DUKE'S ALLIANCE
BOOK TWO

DAWN BROWER

"The Very first moment I beheld him, my heart was irrevocably gone."

— JANE AUSTEN, LOVE AND
FRIENDSHIP

Contents

DEFYING THE DUKE
ARI THATCHER

HER DUKE OF SIN

EXCERPT: A LADY NEVER TELLS

To everyone that believes in love.

<h1 style="text-align:center">Prologue</h1>

As an eligible gentleman of marriageable age George St. Giles, the Duke of Cranbrook was by far one of the most sought after unattached men currently socializing amongst society. He was wealthy and had a title many ladies craved to have attached to their name. That wasn't arrogance on his part. No, it was an unfortunate, or fortunate depending on one's viewpoint, fact of his life.

He enjoyed having a sizeable fortune at his disposal, and his rank afforded him as many luxuries as those funds did. To suggest he wasn't grateful for the good fortune birth allowed him would be ridiculous. George was not a foolish man, and he fully intended to keep all of his faculties. Otherwise, that might prove disastrous.

With all the trappings of wealth at his disposal came as many drawbacks. Women often pressed him for something he could not give them. Most of them hoped for marriage, but some would happily allow him to take them to his bed without the benefit of vows. Their actions were disturbing at best, but definitely disruptive.

He was ready to give up on polite society and hide at his country estate. Cranbrook Castle would be lovely this time of year. Soon, the gardens would bloom, and the maze his father had built would be enshrouded with greenery and luscious vegetation. Few could navigate that maze, and he longed to become lost within it. At least there he'd be safe from probing glances and even more prying hands. He still couldn't quite believe how many women thought it would be all right to grope him.

He sighed.

"What has ye so glum," a man said from behind him. George glanced toward the man and grinned. At least this one person he welcomed readily. The Duke of Allister had recently come into his title, and he had to have observed some of the wantonness of the ladies of the ton of late.

"How long have you been in town?" he asked Allister.

"Long enough tae realize I'd rather be back home in Scotland," he said, with a rich brogue that signified his highland ancestry. "Ah doona know how ye suffer through all of this every day."

"It's a cross I must bear," he told Allister in a grave tone. "You can always return to your beloved highlands. I'm sure the ladies there are not so forthright."

"In that ye be wrong, Yer Grace," he replied, then chuckled. "They're brazen enough, but in different ways, ye ken."

He nodded. "A title is desirable and you're unmarried as yet."

"Aye," Allister replied. "But I won't marry a lass that decides tae warm my bed without invitation. Ye would be forced to be more...honorable."

Somehow, he doubted it was that simple. "If an innocent stripped naked and slid into your bedchamber, her family wouldn't be after your head if you failed to make her your wife?" George lifted a brow.

"They might try tae insist," Allister agreed. "But I won't bloody do anything. I doona wish tae. They all know this and none have been that bold as yet."

"I've narrowly escaped a few well-set marriage traps in the past sennight alone." Every attempt had been a nuisance, and he had to find some way to escape the insanity of it all. "I'm going to retire to Cranbrook Castle soon, but I have to attend to a few important items before I can comfortably do so." He turned toward the duke. An idea suddenly formed in his head. Something that would benefit both of them... "We should form an alliance."

"I thought we were already friendly enough," Allister reminded him. "Why would we need tae make anything so formal?"

How did he explain what he wanted to do? "There are several individuals like ourselves that encounter the same issue." George curated his words carefully. "There are ladies that will do anything to secure the match they desire most. Not all ladies are so...mercenary with their intentions."

"True," Allister said. "And this alliance would do what?"

"It wouldn't be a club. We don't need anything that would that we need to keep formed for every day use. We would form something more unceremonious, an alliance for all those aware of its existence. Simply put... We all would agree to aid another member of our secret alliance should we be called upon to assist them, and if we ever become aware of a ploy to trap one of us into an unwanted union, it would be our duty to warn the intended target."

Allister was quiet for several moments. "No man wishes for such a trap. Marriage should be mutually agreed upon." He tilted his head to the side as if considering all aspects of George's proposal. "Aye. I think this will be excellent. We can protect each other from the wee lasses with wanton purposes." Allister chuckled. "At least the ones that wish tae lead us tae vows we're not read tae say in front of a parson."

"I'm glad you see the wisdom of this endeavor," George said, and then grinned. "We can write up a pact and all sign it. There are a few other individuals I know that would gladly sign as well."

Allister nodded. "I do as well. We can meet at yer estate and discuss it. There will be fewer ears around tae overhear what we wish tae remain undisclosed there."

"So we're agreed." George felt a sense of relief rush through him now that he had a strategy in place to handle all the unwanted attention. It wouldn't solve everything, but it would help with a lot of the schemes in place. "In a fortnight we will meet with the other individual that are to join our alliance at Cranbrook Castle. I'll have a document prepared for us to sign and add any amendments to if they're required. We can use the excuse that we're having a hunting party for our meeting."

"Aye," Allister replied with a quick nod. "I'll be there. Now if ye will pardon my abrupt departure. There's a lass over there that is making me a wee bit nervous. Until we meet again, Yer Grace."

George chuckled as the duke left him alone. He would depart soon as well. The atmosphere had become quite unbearable in the last several minutes. Especially since he no longer had the buffer of the Duke of Allister's company to keep most of the ladies from approaching him. This alliance would work. It had to...

One

Clouds formed overhead, threatening to unleash a torrential rain on those unlucky enough to be caught in the storm. Miss Eleanor Jones would be one of those unfortunate individuals to be drowned in the pelting drops as it fell from the sky. She glanced at the darkness forming above once again and quickened her pace. Cranbrook Castle loomed ahead, and all she had to do was make it to the servants' entrance and she'd be safe from a good soaking. She might not make it. She probably wouldn't make it. Drat.

Eleanor needed that position. How could she present her best self if she was nothing more than a drowned rat dripping all over the castle's elegant interior? That would not leave a good impression with the servants or the residents of the castle. She should run. Perhaps a sweaty brow and gasping for breath would be a better appearance to present them than a soaping wet mess.

She set a faster pace, hoping to outrun the rain. Her directions had been exact. She was to present herself first to the housekeeper, Mrs. Hopson, then she would be introduced to Lady Craven, and if the countess approved, she could begin as the young Earl of Craven's nanny. Eleanor wouldn't have any prospects if she wasn't granted the position. She had the education to teach the young earl, but she had no experience as a governess.

Finally she reached the servants' entrance and rapped on the door harder than she normally would. A light drizzle had started to fall, but that wouldn't last for long. It felt good on her heated skin, though, so she welcomed that mist. The heavy door opened and an older woman stood in the entrance. She had dark hair pulled back in a severe bun and it was peppered with streaks of gray throughout. Her eyes were almost as gray as those strands, too. Her cheeks were ruddy and her body was round and plump. "Who might ye be," she asked in a heavy Scottish brogue. A sure testament at how close they were to the border.

"My name is Miss Eleanor Jones. I'm expected." The woman stared at her for several moments as if she were an undesirable bug she debated squishing beneath her boot. "For the governess position," she stammered out nervously.

"Aye," she said in a firm tone. "I ken who you be. Had to gauge yer grit I did. Come inside before the storm blows ye away."

Eleanor didn't hesitate to enter the castle at the invitation. She didn't want to be in the storm. Especially as the clouds seemed to have darkened even further in the seconds, she stood outside the servants' entrance. "Are you the housekeeper?"

"Nay," she said. "Mrs. Hopson is in with the countess. I'm tae bring ye tae them posthaste."

So she had no intention of introducing herself? Eleanor would find it rude, but she didn't much care what this woman thought of her. She had no say in her employment. There were only two individuals that she had to concern herself with in this interview: the countess and the housekeeper. She would put in more effort once this woman led her to them.

She walked down a long hallway. They passed several maids busy with their daily tasks. A blonde maid folded towels and another polished silverware. Neither of them glanced at her as she kept moving forward behind the stern woman in front of her. Clearly the housekeeper ran a strict household or they would be gossiping at the very least. None of them said one word. It was almost disturbing.

Finally, they reached a pair of doors that swung inward as she pushed them open. Inside was a luxurious sitting room. A set of small mahogany tables flanked two blue velvet settees, and a matching chair sat between settees. A woman with dark hair pulled back into an elegant chignon sat serenely on one of the settees. She held a delicate teacup on one hand as she sipped on the hot liquid. The other woman had dark auburn hair that was pulled back as severely as the woman that escorted Eleanor inside the castle. Her eyes were a rich brown that held little humor in them.

"Pardon the interruption, milady," the woman said from the entrance. "The applicant for the governess position is here tae discuss it with ye."

The countess glanced at her and smiled. "Please come in." She motioned toward the rude lady and said, "That will be all, Ruth. Please return to the kitchen and have a maid bring more biscuits. I'm afraid Mrs. Hopson and I finished them all."

"I'll send a maid straightaway, milady," Ruth told her. At least now Eleanor had a name for the discourteous woman. She rushed to do the countess's bidding and Eleanor breathed a sigh of relief."

"Would you like some tea?" the countess asked her. "Please have a seat." She gestured toward the other settee. "Mrs. Hopson and I were finished discussing the household accounts. I see to them with her for my brother, the duke, since he refuses to marry."

That seemed oddly personal... Perhaps the countess liked to gossip? "Tea would be lovely," she told her. She wouldn't comment on the duke's lack of a wife. That wouldn't be the best way to impress the countess of the housekeeper. Especially if the housekeeper was as strict as she appeared.

The countess poured tea into a cup and handed it to her. She didn't ask her how she took her tea and Eleanor didn't offer the information, either. She'd like sugar, but as that was a luxury she couldn't afford herself, she'd taken to drinking it plain, anyway. She accepted the cup from her and took a sip. "Thank you, my lady."

Mrs. Hopson glanced at her finally. "You don't

have any actual experience as a governess. Yet you come highly recommended. Your references are impeccable." She set down her account book. "Why do you wish to be a governess, Miss. Jones?"

She didn't actually want to be a governess. Eleanor had no choice in the matter. Her father had been a vicar, and one that didn't have the sense to save any funds to bequeath his daughter if he should leave her alone in the world. "I enjoy teaching," she admitted. "I may not have experience as a governess, but I assisted my father with his students. He had a few boys he taught math, Latin, and history too, three times a week. I have benefitted from the same education since I was a young girl."

"Your father was a vicar?" the countess asked.

"He was," Eleanor answered. "He resided in the same parish for over a decade. It was a good income, but he taught to help supplement our needs. Viscount Ranford didn't mind as long as it didn't interfere with my father's primary duties."

"And did it?" Mrs. Hopson asked.

"Interfere?" Eleanor asked. "Not at all. I stepped in with the lessons if my father were to be called away. It's why he ensured I had an excellent education." Truthfully, she'd taught most of those lessons the past few years. Her father had taken ill and could barely complete his vicar duties.

"You don't mind having the one student?" the countess asked. "My son can be...difficult. We have had several governesses quit after a week. We're hoping that you'll have the resilience to handle his disruptive behavior without fleeing."

Was that why Ruth had tried to ascertain her fortitude earlier? "I do not anticipate having any difficulties. He wouldn't be the first boy to test his teacher. I'm certain we will find our way after he realized I won't disappear like all the others."

"Are you afraid of slimy creatures?" Mrs. Hopson asked. "Like frogs."

"No, I am not." Her lips twitched. If the housekeeper knew she'd run wild as a young girl, she wouldn't have to ask that question. "They won't frighten me away."

"Good," the countess said. "Then we shall hire you on a temporary basis. If you withstand the week, we will discuss a permanent position. Let's bring down my son for you to meet."

"I'll retrieve him, my lady," the housekeeper said.

They sat in silence for several moments. Eleanor didn't know how to converse with a proper lady. She'd been around men and boys her entire life. For that reason, she could handle any pranks the young earl sent her way. But this... polite conversation. That was foreign to her. It did not matter that she was fluent in several languages. None of that would aid her now.

Thankfully, she didn't have long to wait. The housekeeper led a small boy no older than seven into the sitting room. He had hair the same shade as his mother's, but his eyes were an ice blue. He must have gotten those striking eyes from his late father.

"This is Elliot Allen, the ninth Earl of Craven," the housekeeper told Eleanor. "Until he gives you leave to use his given name, you will address him as Lord Craven. Is that understood?"

They were going to allow a child to decide if she had to use his title or his given name? She almost shrugged, but somehow refrained. "I understand." There was no other answer to give any of them; however, did they realize they were setting off at a disadvantage? The child may be an earl, but how was she going to teach him when he held all the cards? Somehow, she'd manage it. She had to. This was her last chance at employment. "Hello, Lord

Craven. I'm Miss Jones. We're going to learn a lot together."

"Are we?" He lifted a brow, mocking her. "I give you a day."

With that precarious statement, he turned around and strode out of the room. What a little shite... They would see about that. She would gladly give him a lesson in manners first of all. He might not know it yet, but he'd thrown the gauntlet and Eleanor gladly picked it up. No one bested her. Especially not a little bratty boy who should know better...

She turned toward the countess and pasted a smile on her face. "Your son seems lovely."

She snorted. Actually snorted. "It's kind of you to say that, but I know he's a bloody brat. I do hope you can teach him manners. I've failed to make him realize how important they are. It is why we're living at my brother's home. It is my intention that between you and the duke, he'll be exposed to how polite society interacts with each other. He won't last at Eton if he keeps up this rude behavior."

She expected the duke to help teach her son manners? At least she realized the boy was rude. Some parents thought their child could do nothing wrong. "I believe that can be done. It won't happen immediately, though. It will take time for the necessity to absorb into that mind of his. He's too used to having his way, it seems." She wouldn't have been so honest if the countess hadn't done so first. "But once I have a plan in place, I need you to follow it too. It won't work if you give in to every one of his demands."

The housekeeper grinned. It was the first time Mrs. Hopson had shown any emotion. "I believe I've said as much."

"Yes, you have." Lady Craven sighed. "Outline your lessons and we will discuss them. Once we decide on what to do, I will follow them, and I'll ensure the staff and my brother do as well. Elliot needs consistency more than anything. I grieved for his father too long and now we're all paying a heavy toll for my lack of discipline."

"It's not too late, my lady." She met her gaze and smiled softly. "He can unlearn undesirable behaviors in much the way he learned them to begin with. We'll have him on the right path in time. You just need to be patient."

"I will," she said. "I have no choice."

That's ironic. Eleanor had believed the same thing when she approached Cranbrook Castle. Now she felt a little lighter. This was where she needed to be, and she'd make a wonderful governess. She felt light for the first time in days, no weeks. Finally, fortune smiled upon her. She wouldn't waste this opportunity. It might be her last chance at creating a life for herself.

Two

Two months later...

The carriage hit a bump in the road and sent George into the side. His head bounced off lightly and he groaned. He hated traveling, but unfortunately this trip was necessary. He was returning home. No, that wasn't the truth. He was running. His meeting with the Duke of Allister may have wrapped his reasons for returning to Cranbrook Castle into a tidy bow, but he knew the truth. The last thing he wanted to do was return home to escape marriage minded misses from sinking their claws into him.

He didn't want to be trapped into marriage. If he were to be honest, he didn't know if he would ever want to marry. Yes, one day he would have to find a wife, but he aimed for that to be on his own terms. He *should* marry sooner rather than later. Then he would be done with that chore, but he couldn't find it in himself to bind himself a woman yet. There was nothing convenient about marriage, and if he leapt into one, it would become something unbearable.

The carriage turned and started the long trek down the drive to Cranbrook Castle. Soon it would stop and he'd finally be able to escape the confines of the carriage and he could walk inside his home. His sister had the run of the castle and he had left it willingly in her capable hands. Ever since her husband died, she had come to live at Cranbrook. The eighth Earl of Craven had left his estate nearly destitute. George had taken over overseeing the estate, so when his nephew came of age, he wouldn't have any funds to take care of his proper-ties. Part of ensuring that meant downsizing the household expenses and therefore eliminating any unnecessary staff. There had only been one solution, and it required his sister and nephew to reside with him.

That had been a year earlier. Now the estate was starting to produce income again, and by the time his nephew was ready to attend Eton, it should be more than prosperous. His sister could stay at Cranbrook or she could return to Craven Abbey. He would leave the decision up to her.

Now, though… He had other considerations to make. If he did marry, where would that leave his sister? She'd had control over the castle for a year now. Would she resent the new duchess once he married? He hoped not. Of course, this all depended on him finding a woman he wanted to marry. That was unlikely to happen soon. Especially since he fully planned on remaining at Cranbrook for a couple of months. The chances of him finding a bride at his own home was quite unlikely. That was the entire reason he'd decided to return to the castle. He needed that very reprieve.

The carriage came to a stop. He took a deep breath, then pushed open the door. He didn't need the footman to open it for him. George was more than ready to exit, and he didn't wish to wait a second longer than necessary. The servants would see to his trunks. He strode to the entrance and walked inside. No one was there to greet him, and he wasn't sure if that bothered him or not. He had sent word he would be returning. Where was everyone?

As if on cue, a boy came barreling through the foyer and collided into him. George groaned, but grabbed his nephew and set him in front of him. "Elliot," he said sternly. "Are you supposed to be running through the house?"

"I had to," Elliot insisted. "You don't understand."

He closed his eyes briefly and prayed for patience. "Then please explain it to me."

Elliot was a handful, and he thought his sister had hired a governess that could handle his willful nature. Clearly, that hadn't been the case. Not if his current actions had anything to recommend the woman. She clearly didn't know what she was doing.

A few seconds later a woman strode into the foyer, a little out of breath, and a little irritated. Strands of blonde hair framed her face. Not by design, but because they had clearly escaped from the stern bun she had fashioned them into earlier that day. She had high cheekbones and a perfectly bow shaped mouth that had been designed for kisses. Her eyes were a pale blue that would resemble ice on a cold winter day, but sent heat straight through him. A mixture of fire and ice that burned—he had never been so intrigued at first sight. Who was this woman?

She wiped her hands over her dark blue skirt

and focused all of her attention on Elliot. "Lord Craven," she said sternly. "Do I need to remind you that you should not be running in the halls?"

He pushed up his chin defiantly and said, "And do I need to remind you that you are a servant? You do what I say."

George rolled his eyes. This nonsense had to stop now. Perhaps it was good that he had returned to the castle. Elliot needed to learn more than mere manners. He had to learn how to treat people, servant or not. No one should be disrespected. He cleared his throat. "You must be the new governess."

Elliot tilted his head to the side and grinned. It was something almost evil and George didn't like it. "Now you're going to understand. My uncle is home and you're going to have to listen. He's a duke."

Bloody hell... The pretty governess lifted her gaze to his. His gut clenched, and he lost all ability to breathe. Without saying one word, she said more than he knew possible, and damned if he didn't want to uncover everything about her.

❦

ELEANOR HAD BEEN THE EARL OF CRAVEN'S GOVERNESS for a mere week, and she was failing. She thought she could handle him, and for the most part, she had. That didn't mean that she didn't have to fight for every bit of ground she gained or that he listened. He refused to sit still for longer than a few moments and then took off if she was distracted, even for a little bit.

And now the duke was home...

She hadn't even glanced at the man when she had come into the room. Her attention had been solely focused on the little brat that had continued to make her life hell. Now that she had taken the time to glance at him, she lost all ability to think or form words. She had never seen a more gorgeous man in her entire life. His hair was dark as a night sky devoid of moonlight and his eyes were like spun gold shimmering in candlelight. There were some specks of green in that gold that made her think of grass on a warm, sunny day.

Eleanor swallowed the lump in her throat. What should she do? Slowly, her brain started to form thoughts again. She'd never felt like a ninny before, but this man had turned her into one with just one glance. How was she going to get anything done with a man so handsome she lost the ability to use the intelligence god had gifted to her? "Your Grace," she said, and curtsied. "My apologies for our interruption."

He chuckled lightly. It was like pouring warm honey sliding over her tongue. Sinfully decadent, and highly irresistible... "I do not believe you are the one at fault." He glanced down at his nephew. "Do you want to explain yourself?" The duke lifted a brow and waited.

"Uncle..." the earl began, but clearly he hadn't thought the duke would take Eleanor's side. In her estimation, that made him even better than she could have imagined. Not many dukes would care about a servant.

"Don't give me any excuses," the duke warned his nephew. "You were running. Something I have told you not to do myself. So tell me. Why are you misbehaving now?"

The earl glanced down and shuffled his feet. "I don't know."

"You don't?" The duke frowned. "Then I believe you owe..." He glanced at her. "I owe you an apology, too. I'm afraid I do not know your name."

"It's Miss Jones," the young earl informed the duke. "She's my new governess."

The duke smiled. "I gathered that much." He nodded in her direction. "You owe Miss Jones an apology. I'm home now and I expect you to behave properly and learn. If you're ever to be a proper lord and run your estate, you need to have an excellent education. Do you understand me?"

The young earl nodded. He turned to her and said. "Please forgive me, Miss Jones. I promise I won't run from my lessons again. I'm sorry for being difficult."

With that turn around he wished the duke had been in residence from the beginning. It was clear Lord Craven respected him far more than he did anyone else. Would he return to such improper behavior once the duke returned to London? All she could do was pray that once he did, she would have gained some respect from the young earl before-hand. "Apology accepted," she told him. "We should return to the schoolroom now. Your uncle has only arrived, and he probably wishes to have some time to himself after such a long journey."

"Are you staying for a while?" the earl asked his uncle.

He seemed anxious for this answer. She hoped that the duke would stay, not only for herself but also for the boy. He clearly needed the attention from his uncle. "Yes," he told him. "I'm here for at least a month. Now run along. You have many things to learn."

The boy nodded and walked back to the schoolroom. Eleanor smiled, then glanced up at the duke. "Thank you, Your Grace," she said.

He held her gaze. "Think nothing of it."

Her heart skipped a beat as he stared at her. What should she say? There didn't seem like there was anything else to add, but she didn't want this time to end. Eleanor was a fool. The duke had far better things to do with his time than entertain a silly governess. "Good afternoon." She turned away from him and went to attend to her charge in the schoolroom.

"Miss Jones," the duke called to her.

Eleanor stopped and glanced back at him. "Yes?"

"After you are done with today's lessons, I would like to speak with you. Come see me in my study."

She gulped in air like a fish out of water. Hell. Had she messed up far more than she had realized? What would she do if he turned her away, and she was forced to find another position? This one had been her last hope.

"Yes, Your Grace," she said, then turned away. She couldn't look at him a second longer. Her heart thudded heavily inside her chest, and just not from the fear she might be sacked. He made her wish for things she had no right to. He would never want anything with her. No duke would look at a governess and want more. Duke's did not marry a penniless vicar's daughters that had to seek employment to survive, and she would never be a mistress.

It was too bad she had morals or she might throw herself at the handsome Duke of Cranbrook and do something far too scandalous for her own good... She sighed. Eleanor couldn't escape the truth. She would never have a family, and the Duke of Cranbrook would marry someone else. He had to think of his line, and he wouldn't choose her to be his duchess. Her fate held something far different, and less pleasant, and she had to accept that.

He wasn't for her, no matter how much she wished she could change it. She couldn't make him love her, and she didn't even know if she would if that option was open to her. Just because he was heavenly to gaze upon didn't make him a good choice for a husband. She had to push those thoughts away and do the job she was hired for, and leave dreams for those that had the luxury of wallowing in them.

Three

George sat at his desk and stared at the ledgers, demanding his attention. He couldn't focus on anything that his estate manager had written in them. All he could think about was a certain beguiling governess and his desire to spend more time in her company. She hadn't said or done anything that would indicate she had any interest in him, and that in itself was appealing. All females, save his family, showered him with attention. The title put ideas inside their heads and most of it could not be interpreted as good ones either.

Such was his cross to bear as a duke...

That wasn't arrogance, though he did have his fair share of that. George knew his worth both in title and wealth. Not all dukes were created equal, as was the case of most gentry. His title was old and his wealth extensive. That made him far more desirable than many of the gentlemen in the ton. Which brought him back to the conundrum that had chased him from London to the safety of his countryseat.

He scrubbed his hands over his face. These thoughts were doing nothing to solve his current dilemma. He had to go over those ledgers and stop thinking about his nephew's governess.

"Ye look like a troubled man." That familiar Scottish brogue made George smile.

He glanced up at the Duke of Allister and grinned. "Why are you here?" George lifted a brow. "Isn't your own estates keeping you busy?"

Allister's lips twitched. "Aye, they are." He strolled over to the chair near George's desk and sat. "But I do believe we have some things tae discuss."

"Is that so," George said, then frowned. "Is this about our little alliance?"

"Aye," Allister told him. "There is interest and I think it is time tae move forward."

When they had discussed having an informal group that helped others avoid marriage, George had thought it a great idea. It was, in theory, a way for a gentleman to remain a bachelor until he chose to find a wife. He wasn't so certain what he wanted anymore. "Have you organized everything?" He should have taken a more active role, but he had been so preoccupied.

The Duke of Allister set down a parchment on his desk. "This outlines everything. I think ye should keep our informal charter here. It was yer idea, after all."

George lifted the parchment and scanned the information there. Allister had been thorough. It was signed by several other dukes and heirs to dukedoms. Not all of them were currently unwed, but they wanted to support any gentleman that found themselves in need. He lifted his own quill and signed his name to the agreement. "Then it is settled."

"Aye," Allister said. "I think anyone that might have an interest in our alliance has been apprised of it. The secrecy of it will remain the key tae our success. Will ye keep the contract safe?"

George nodded. "I will." Then he opened a locked drawer in his desk and placed it inside. Once the turned the key in the lock, he returned his attention back to Allister. "I will put it in a more secure place later, but this will do for now."

Allister nodded. "A locked drawer is far better than leaving it unattended on yer desk."

He smiled. "True," he replied. "Would you care for a drink?" George could certainly use one.

"As long as ye have a wee bit of whisky fer me tae enjoy, I will not say no."

George shook his head and held back a smile. "I keep that on hand just for you, Your Grace." He laughed. "I refuse to drink that rot." He preferred brandy and only drank whisky when he wanted his throat to burn for days...which was nearly never.

"Ye have no taste," Allister told him.

"We will have to agree to disagree on that," George told him as he handed him a glass of whisky. He held up his glass of brandy. "To our newest venture."

"May it ever be successful," Allister agreed. They both took a drink of their liquor and grinned. "Ye did see a bit preoccupied when I arrived. What has ye so concerned?"

"Nothing concern yourself with," George told him. He didn't want to explain himself to his friend. What would he think of George's obsession with the new governess in residence? He would likely think that George had lost his bloody mind. "My mind wandered a bit, and I had trouble concentrating on the accounts."

"Then perhaps ye should take some time away from them. Clear yer mind and when ye return tae them, they'll be waiting for yer attention. Sometimes all a person needs is time away from the things that they cannot discern tae understand what needs tae be done."

That could work for a lot of things that George had on his mind. "Perhaps you are right." He could take a ride and then return to his study and the ennui of his ledgers. What did he have to lose? "Are you in a hurry to return to your own estate?"

Allister shook his head. "No. What did ye wish tae do?"

"I'm going for a ride," George told him. "If you wish to join me, I'd appreciate the company."

"Why don't we do more than that," Allister told him. "We should go into town and find us a bit of sport."

"A game?" George lifted a brow.

"That," Allister agreed. "Perhaps more if the opportunity presents itself."

George didn't want to find a woman to warm his bed, if that was what Allister was suggesting. A game of cards would be distracting enough, though.

"Why don't we ride to town and see if there is anything interesting? If not, I'll return home, and you can do the same."

"Agreed," Allister said. "Lets be off then."

George stood and headed out of his study with Allister on his heels. They walked to the stable and had their horses prepared for the ride to town. George only hoped he wouldn't regret this decision.

ELEANOR HAD THE AFTERNOON OFF TO DO WHATEVER SHE wished. It was her half day off and she planned on enjoying it. Her charge was in the care of his mother, and Eleanor could breathe. It had been challenging at best, at worst, she had almost given up and walked away. Even though she needed this position, she wondered if being a governess was where she belonged. She liked learning, but teaching... Some things a person just wasn't good at, and she wondered if teaching was beyond her.

It could just be her charge. It could be her. How was she to know which it was and how did she fix any of it? Eleanor sighed and wandered through the garden. She had found a secluded area of the extensive gardens and sat down to read. The afternoon sun beat down on her and warmed her skin. She should have found some shade, but she enjoyed the sunlight. Besides, if she failed at being a governess, she didn't know how many moments of leisure she might have.

It also didn't help that she found the Duke of Cranbrook utterly fascinating. Fantasizing about that man was not going to help her. If he found out that she dreamed about being his... She would be sacked without a reference. A governess had no place desiring to be anything to the duke. If she allowed herself, she could easily imagine she was in love with him. His kindness did not mean he returned her feelings and she best remember that.

At least she knew he would continue to treat her with respect. Eleanor was lucky there. Some gentlemen believed servants beneath them and unnoticeable. The Duke of Cranbrook seemed to know every single one of his servants. They were all treated well and that loyalty they showed him was well earned. He was a good man. Was it any wonder why she thought herself in love with the man?

She had been lounging in her little area of the garden for some time now. The sun was starting to set and she should return to the house. But once she left her spot in the garden, she would have to return to reality. Something Eleanor was loath to do...

"Bloody hell," a gentleman muttered.

Eleanor sat up. Who was there? Should she announce herself or hide? This was not the first time she had secluded herself in this particular spot in the garden. No one ever came here. Yet, someone had, and that left her too startled to react.

"How can I be lost in my own damn garden," the gentleman mumbled.

It was the duke... He sounded...wrong. Should she help him? He was mumbling something, but she couldn't quite make it out. Slowly, Eleanor got to her feet and tiptoed toward the sounds of his feet shuffling against the stone path. "Your Grace," she called out to him.

The Duke of Cranbrook stiffened and turned toward her. The duke narrowed his gaze, as if he couldn't quite see her properly. "The delightful governess?" He took a step toward her. "Am I imagining you?"

He was inebriated. She had never been around a man who was foxed before. What should she do? "I'm quite real, Your Grace."

The duke took a few steps toward her. He reached out his hand and grazed the back of his hand over her cheek. "So soft," he said in a hoarse tone. "So, so lovely."

Her cheeks heated at his words. Surely he didn't realize he was talking to her. Eleanor had never been so captivated in her entire life. She should not allow him to take such liberties. She had a reputation to preserve, and yet, she also wanted him to do so much more than merely touch his hand to her cheek. "Do you require assistance, Your Grace?"

"I do," he said, then groaned. "But I shouldn't ask that of you. You're far too sweet, lovely governess." He tilted his head to the side. "Do you taste as sweet as you look? I bet you do." The duke shook his head, then groaned again. "Shouldn't have done that. Now the world is spinning before me."

Eleanor sighed. He was saying things she longed to hear, but clearly the man had too much to drink and she shouldn't take any of it seriously. He might say those things to any female he stumbled across. "Let me help you back to the castle, Your Grace." She stepped toward him.

That was her first mistake. She tripped and fell into him, then they both tumbled to the ground. The duke had wrapped his arms around her and braced them both so that when they hit the ground; he cushioned her fall. "If you wanted me to hold you, all you had to do was ask. No need to throw yourself into my arms. I assure you, I am quite willing. At least with you…only you."

Did he think she was someone else? That was the only thing that made any lick of sense. "We should return to the castle, Your Grace?"

"I like it here," he insisted. "Here I have you. At the castle, I have to pretend I don't want you. Don't leave me."

"Your Grace…"

"George," the duke said. "You must call me George. We're more than mere acquaintances now. I've held you, touched you, and I damn well plan on kissing you."

"I cannot…" She didn't get the chance to finish that sentence. He was a man of his word and he pressed his lips to hers. She lost all ability to think or form words. All she could do was feel, and that kiss sent a spike of desire through her entire being.

Eleanor never imagined a kiss could make her feel so damn much, or that she would suddenly want far more than she ever should. Before, it was a dream. This was reality, and reality far surpassed anything she could ever have imagined. This kiss. It was everything. How would she ever return to being a mere governess after this?

Four

George groaned and placed his hand over his aching head. He should never have listened to Allister and gone into town. Then he wouldn't have imbibed too much and... He cursed and sat up abruptly. What had he done? Surely he couldn't be recalling things correctly. When he returned, he definitely had not wandered into the garden and he most definitely had not kissed the governess.

He cursed again.

As much as he wanted to be wrong, he was also certain he did remember the previous evening correctly. He had kissed her, and it had been a glorious kiss at that. She hadn't pushed him away, and she had let him thoroughly taste that delectable mouth of hers. But everything after that had gone sideways. She had stepped away from him, and then she had insisted that she help him inside. Once they reached the castle, another servant had appeared and ran to fetch George's valet.

Bivens had taken charge immediately, and he had lost any chance he had of seducing the lovely governess. He should be thankful for that. Seducing the lovely Miss Jones would have been a mistake; however, he couldn't find any semblance of gratefulness. To his addled brain, it was nothing more than a missed opportunity. He wanted her, and damn the consequences. Though there still might be some of those to contend with. She could still resign her position and she had every right to do so.

George had to make it right with her…

He just didn't know how to go about accomplishing that particular feat. Bivens strolled into his bedchamber and stared at him. The disapproval in his valet's eyes was evident as he glared at George. "Your Grace," he greeted him. His tone was far more neutral than his gaze implied. "I've had a bath drawn for you. I'm also to tell you we have guests in the drawing room, and Lady Craven has requested you join her at your earliest opportunity."

He groaned. Again. Who the blazes had decided

to visit Cranbrook Castle? At least Allister had made sense. His estate was only a half day's ride, and they had important issues to discuss. No one else should have cause to pay a call on them. It was the sole reason he had decided to abandon London for the peace of his countryseat. Now it appeared as if that solitude would be intruded upon as well.

"Did she mention who is visiting?" Perhaps it wasn't as terrible as he anticipated it would be. He'd been wrong before, and he desperately wanted his assumptions to be incorrect.

"She did not," Bivens said. He remained still near the entrance to George's dressing room. "I am merely delivering the message I was given."

Of course he was. George's sister never gave details to the servants. She didn't believe there was a reason to, and there probably wasn't. That didn't mean he had to like it. He preferred to be prepared for anything, but his sister wasn't going to allow him that small comfort. He sighed and strode to the tub. He'd have to bathe quickly or there was no telling what his sister might do. She could be relentless when she demanded someone to do something, and she seemed to think that he needed to be present with this visitation. She rarely requested that of him.

He slid into the warm bath and took a deep, fortifying breath. The bath felt heavenly, and he was glad his valet had arranged it. He might feel more himself after its conclusion, and he would need to be his best before he left his bedchamber. If his sister asked him to join her, then the visitor was one she didn't wish to be alone with for too long.

After he was finished washing, he rose from the water and dried off. Bivens was there, ready to help him dress. He didn't think much as he slid his clothes on and prepared for his day. Dressing was a normal, everyday occurrence, and it didn't deserve any more attention than necessary.

"Where there be anything else, Your Grace?" Bivens asked.

He shook his head. "No. I suppose it is time to join the countess in greeting our guest." Was it too much to hope they left sooner rather than later? He really hoped they didn't intend to stay more than a few hours at most. His worst fear was that they would stay much longer than that. Like overnight...

George didn't wait for his valet to respond. He hadn't really been addressing him, anyway. It was more a rhetorical question that he already knew the answer to. He strolled out of his bedchamber and went to the drawing room. He wondered why his sister had gone there instead of her sitting room, but he didn't stop to ponder it too much. His sister always had a reason for everything she did. That reason wasn't always evident, but he supposed he might be able to discern the truth once he knew the guest's identity.

He stepped toward the entrance of the drawing room and froze. The voices he heard from the other side of the door filled him with dread. His sister's insistence made sense now. What had that infernal woman told her? He closed his eyes and took a deep breath. He should join them, but he couldn't. Not yet, at least. He didn't know what he should do, and he needed time to consider everything first. Lady Felicity Abbot had tried to force him to marry her. She'd set up a scene that would have accomplished that goal. If he had fallen into her trap, she might very well be his duchess now. Thankfully, Allister had rescued him from such a fate.

That didn't mean she hadn't devised a new scheme, and he had to squash it before it took root. There was only one true way for him to escape such a fate. He had to find a wife, and fast. One he chose. Not one that trapped him into such a union. Now he just had to find a woman he wanted to be his bride, and fast.

ELEANOR SAT IN THE GARDEN AND THOUGHT ABOUT THE previous day. He'd kissed her. She doubted he would have if not for his inebriated state, but she couldn't erase that moment from her mind. Nor did she want to. She might never experience anything as pleasurable as that kiss had been ever again. It was the single most satisfying moment of her life. Nothing would induce her to forget it. Nothing. She would relive that moment to her dying day.

She might never have him, or his love, but she had that kiss. He might not remember it, but that was all right. She could remember it for the both of them. After all, it wasn't as if she had any suitors or a reason to let go of the dream of him.

Eleanor headed to a nearby bench. Her charge, the Earl of Craven, didn't feel well and was in the nursery being taken care of by his nanny. He had a little cough, and the countess was concerned it might develop into something more serious. That development had given her the morning to herself. If the young earl was feeling better later, they would resume his lessons. For now, she was going to enjoy her morning. That meant a long stroll in the garden and perhaps a little daydreaming, too.

Footsteps from the opposite direction caught her attention. Someone else was in the garden. It was probably one of the gardeners. The countess had a guest, and she overheard one of the maids telling the duke's valet that his presence was requested. That was too bad. She would have loved to see the duke again. In the garden. For another kiss...

There goes that fantasizing again...

She sighed. Eleanor would not be so lucky twice in as many days. She had to keep her reminding herself of one fact. The duke was not for her. He would never offer for her. He would never truly be hers.

A man rounded the corner and collided with Eleanor. She lost her balance and began to fall backwards. The gentleman pulled her forward, and she landed instead in his arms. It seemed as if she was going to repeat what had happened the day before. The difference, of course, was that this time she hadn't fallen to the ground, and the duke was not inebriated.

"My apologies, Miss Jones." The duke stared at her intently. "I should have been paying attention to where I walked. Are you all right?"

He didn't seem any worse for the wear... Perhaps drinking too much brandy didn't affect him as it did others. "Do not fret, Your Grace," she told him. "No harm was done." He'd given her permission to use his given name but she couldn't bring herself to do it. Especially since he still remained formal with her. Surely he didn't recall granting her that privilege, and even if he had, perhaps he regretted it. She would not take advantage of his inebriated state and take liberties he normally would not have given her.

"I fear there is much I need to apologize for," he told her, his tone grave. "The state I was in yesterday…" He cleared his throat. His golden eyes were filled with sincerity as he spoke. The duke felt guilty it seemed… "I must assure you I do not normally imbibe too much and take advantage of innocents. You may remain assured that I will not take liberties with your person again."

Her heart sank. She'd been right about one thing. He did regret kissing her. What should she say? Should she brush it aside as nothing or be honest? What did she have to lose? Only everything… Eleanor took a deep breath and pushed her disappointment down. She pasted a smile on her face and met his gaze. "I never thought you were anything more than a gentleman, Your Grace. You needn't concern yourself about my welfare. I'm all right with what happened between us." She wouldn't come out and tell him that his kiss had changed something inside of her, but she didn't wish for him to think she regretted it either.

"You don't think ill of me?" He lifted a brow. "I'm the worst sort of scoundrel for what I did."

"Are you?" She tilted her head to the side. "That is not how I view you."

He nodded a little absentmindedly. "You're too kind to me, Miss Jones. I do not deserve your good charity."

The duke might view himself unfavorably; however, she could not look at him as anything but a man with integrity. Other gentlemen might not even acknowledge her, let alone apologize for their actions. Instead of speaking about that kiss and his intentions any longer, she chose to broach another topic with him. "I've heard we have guests. Have they already departed?"

He scowled. "I don't believe that anyone has left Cranbrook Castle. As much as I would like to ignore them, I should quit being a coward and go face them."

"You do not care for Lady Craven's guest?" Who had come to visit and why did he look at them disparagingly?

"Lady Felicity Abbot has arrived." He had a sour

expression on his face that almost made Eleanor giggle. He truly didn't like them. "Lady Felicity fancies herself to be my future duchess. She is quite mistaken in that assumption."

She already hated the woman just for that. Eleanor knew it was unreasonable, but that feeling wouldn't go away. She already thought of George, the duke, as hers. Even though deep down she knew it could never be true. "I see," she said quietly.

"Do you," he said. "I don't. I think she's a loathsome woman." The duke shuddered. "I don't suppose you would marry me and save me from her nefarious intentions." She stared at him, struck mute. Surely he hadn't just asked her to be his wife. She had to have misheard. He blew out a breath. "I know it is too much to ask. Don't answer me. I was foolish to even suggest it. I just know she's here with some scheme and I wanted to avoid the scandal that would eventually arise from it."

He wanted her to save him. How could she say no to that? Did he even understand what it would mean, though? "Your Grace," she began. "Do you really wish me to marry you? Are you jesting?"

He stilled and met her gaze, then his lips tilted upward. That smile sent shivers down his spine. "You're considering it?"

"I don't know…" She stumbled over the words. "That's not a light decision to make. Marriage is forever. Are you certain this is what you want?" She was a fool, but damn it, she would gladly tumble toward that recklessness if it meant he would be hers. Forever. "Why do you want to marry me?"

"Because you're the only woman I want," he told her. "And you're also the one woman that isn't throwing herself at me, demanding something from me. I think we would make a good match." He frowned. "I'm bumbling this and never would have asked. At least not yet…" The duke sighed. "I had hoped we would have more time, but Lady Felicity's arrival changes everything. Please say yes."

He'd wanted more time… She should say no. Eleanor never acted rashly, but this duke… It couldn't be real, but yet, it seemed he really did want her. "All right…" She swallowed the lump that had formed in her throat. "Yes. I will marry you."

She prayed she hadn't just made a terrible mistake.

Five

George could not believe she'd said yes. Were they about to make a grave error in judgement? He couldn't be certain, but he did know one thing with certainty. He wanted her, and marrying her solved so many of his problems. No other woman would be able to trap him into marriage. He would have a duchess, and he had a wife he chose. One he wanted above any other.

"I'd like to marry immediately," he told her. "Today."

She blinked several times before replying. "Today?" Miss Jones tilted her head to the side. "Why?"

He smiled. With this, he could answer without

reservations. "Because I do not wish to wait to make you mine." He'd desired her from the very first moment he'd gazed upon her beautiful face. She'd beguiled him with a mere smile, and now he had to have her. "We can ride to Scotland. The Duke of Allister will gladly act as our witness."

This was all very rushed. George was more aware of that fact than he wanted to admit, but he also didn't care. Once he made a decision, he didn't question it. They could be at Allister's estate in half a day and be wed before nightfall. He would leave a note with Bivens to give to his sister once they departed. George would not risk anything preventing him from reaching his goal. Miss Jones would be the Duchess of Cranbrook before the day was done.

"But..." She nibbled on her bottom lip. "I have duties."

"Don't worry about anything. My nephew will be fine without you." He would have to find a new governess for Elliot. George should feel guilty for stealing Miss Jones from him though he couldn't muster any. She would be his wife, and that was all that mattered to him in this moment. "I promise you, no one will question anything. I'll take care of you and everything else. Do you trust me?"

She nodded. "We'll stay overnight." Miss Jones met his gaze. "In Scotland?"

"Yes," he told her. George could barely hold back the grin that wanted to fill his face. He still couldn't believe she'd said yes. Any other woman he wouldn't have questioned it. Miss Jones seemed different to him, and always had. It didn't matter that they hadn't known each other long. She kept herself apart from him and remained stoic in her duties. That didn't mean she didn't want him. That kiss had revealed much. "I'll arrange for the carriage. Can you meet me in an hour? Don't say a word to anyone. Pack what you need in a valise and we will be off. I'll arrange the rest."

"I can do that." She didn't seem convinced of the wisdom of this plan. He prayed that she wouldn't breathe a word to anyone. They were eloping after all, and George wanted to avoid a certain lady as well. This would work. He would be free of the ladies vying to be his duchess, and he'd be able to claim his governess. Miss Jones glanced at him. "I don't need a full hour. We can leave sooner if you arrange it."

He had never been so motivated in his life. George resisted the urge to kiss her. She was so delectable. "Then it shall be done. I'll ensure it is."

This time he didn't hold back the grin. "I recall I gave you leave to use my given name. Will you not do the same for me?"

Her smile was almost shy as she stared up at him. "Of course," she readily agreed. "Please call me Eleanor."

"No," he told her firmly. "You're my Ellie. Only I will call you that." He leaned down and pressed his lips to hers in one quick kiss. George couldn't stop himself. He'd craved the taste of her lips since that first time. He couldn't forget her, even if he wanted to. She was branded on his skin and he would ensure that she felt the same about him.

"All right," she readily agreed. "You may call me Ellie." She stepped out of his arms and put some distance between them. "But if we are to be wed today, I must depart now or we will never leave. That is, if you still wish to marry me."

"I have not changed my mind in the mere moments since you agreed. I promise that will never happen." Her lovely features brightened as he spoke. "You will be my wife, and I intend to say our vows this evening. You may hold me to that."

"Then I'll join you in a quarter hour. The carriage best be ready for our journey, then." With those words, she spun on her heels and headed back toward the castle. She'd said yes. They were going to wed. Now all he had to do was have the carriage prepared and avoid his sister. That shouldn't be too difficult.

George rushed up to his room and packed a few things. He wrote a quick missive and left it on his writing desk, then rushed to the stables. He didn't have time to dawdle. Once he was at the stable, he ordered a carriage to be prepared. He supervised as the horses were secured to the carriage. A footman and his driver were sent for, and just as everything was being finished, Ellie came strolling forward. Her blonde hair was windswept and her pale blue eyes sparkled with mischief, or was that happiness. George couldn't be certain. Either way, it made her even more lovely to gaze upon.

"Are you ready?" he asked her.

"I've never been more ready for anything in my life," she answered. "Let's get married."

He helped her into the carriage, and then, without any preamble, they were off. Allister would be surprised to see them, but that was all right. The Duke of Allister was a friend and would aid him. The rest would fall into place, and soon he would be a married man. When he returned to Cranbrook he'd have his duchess, and he could send their impromptu visitors away without thinking twice about it.

THE CARRIAGE ROLLED TO A STOP AT THE DUKE OF Allister's estate. It was a large castle, far more foreboding than Cranbrook. Eleanor preferred the quiet elegance of Cranbrook over this estate. Allister's estate spoke volumes about what it had endured over the years. It was a dark fortress designed to withstand any battle, and it had.

George helped her out of the carriage and then walked by her side as they strolled up the stairs to the castle. The door opened before they had time to pick up the knocker and rap the door. A large burly man with snow white hair and stormy gray eyes greeted them. "Good evenin' Yer Grace. Please come inside. The wee lass looks exhausted."

"Is he in?" George asked. He must have meant the Duke of Allister. Eleanor had never met him, but clearly they were good friends. This large man knew him and hadn't questioned his arrival.

"Aye," the burly man said. "He's in his study. Do ye wish fer me tae announce ye?"

George shook his head. "I'll see my way there,

Calum. I have a favor to ask him. Could you have someone bring refreshments? It's been a long journey."

"Aye," the man said. "I'll have Mrs. Andrews bring in a tray. His Grace probably needs something as well."

With those words, Calum left them alone in the foyer. George turned to her and held out his arm to her. "Please come with me to meet my friend. I do believe he'll like you."

And what if he didn't? Would George change his mind about marrying her? She prayed he wouldn't, but this entire marriage idea was impulsive. Eleanor wouldn't blame him if he did reconsider. They could return to Cranbrook and forget about the entire thing. Of course, she would lose her position and she would have to find a new position... She couldn't think about that possibility. Besides, she had to have faith. George said he wouldn't change his mind. He wanted to marry her, and in fact, had seemed excited to do so.

They walked down a long hallway. This castle seemed so dark and dreary. She would hate to live there, but at the same time, there was something appealing about it. Eleanor knew little about Scottish architecture. She would have to see if there were any books about it and study a bit. She had always enjoyed learning about new things. Why should this be any different?

Finally, they reached a doorway. George rapped on the large door and opened it without waiting for permission to enter. A man sat at a large wood desk with his gaze focused on some ledgers before him. He glanced up when they entered, and his smile widened when his gaze met George's. "What brings ye here?"

"I'm here for a wedding," George answered.

"Is that so?" The Duke of Allister rose and walked toward him. "And what wedding are ye here for?"

"Mine," George answered. He pulled her forward and gestured toward her with a nod of his head. "This is my intended. Miss Eleanor Jones, I'd like you to meet The Duke of Allister, one of my closest friends."

Allister frowned. "Ye didn't mention anything about this wee lass when we spoke yesterday. When did this happy development occur?"

"Today," George told him. "There is much I need to tell you, but first, can you help arrange a wedding today? We don't need anything elaborate. I just want to ensure we are wed before we return home tomorrow."

"That can be arranged. A simple wedding can be done here. As long as ye both are ready and willing to admit to yer intention to wed." He met Eleanor's gaze. "Is that yer wish, lass? Do ye want to marry this curmudgeon?"

"I don't find him particularly bad tempered," Eleanor replied softly. "He's more than wonderful and I'd be honored to be his wife."

"Yer a sweet lass, aren't ye," the Duke of Allister said. He didn't seem as if he expected her to reply. He returned his attention back to George. "I'll speak with the preacher and arrange everything."

A maid walked in with a tray filled with biscuits, tiny cakes, and a full tea service. She set it down on the desk and turned toward the Duke of Allister. "Do ye wish me tae serve, Yer Grace?"

"No," Allister replied. "We can see tae it ourselves. Go and tell the cook that we have guests fer dinner. She'll want tae have time tae prepare something special. It appears we are tae have a wedding."

"I'll let her know," the maid said, then curtsied. She left them alone and went to do the task assigned to her.

Allister turned back to them. "Have some tea and cakes," he told them. "I'll go and make the arrangements. I shouldn't be long."

After that, he left George and Eleanor alone. Her stomach filled with dancing butterflies determined to make it impossible for her to eat anything. The biscuits and cakes looked delicious, but she feared she wouldn't be able to keep any of it down. "I'll just have some tea."

"You should eat," George told her.

"I'm not hungry," she argued. "Tea is enough."

She prayed he didn't try to convince her to eat something. Eleanor didn't want to explain why she didn't want any food. She would eat something later. After the wedding... At least she hoped she would be able to eat. There was also the wedding night to consider. She didn't have a mother to explain any of it to her. What if she did something wrong, and he decided he'd made a mistake? Who could she even ask about such things? Eleanor hated being unprepared.

She poured some tea and took a sip. She didn't like sugar or milk in her tea. "Would you like me to pour a cup for you?"

George shook his head. "I'm not in the mood for

tea." He stepped closer to her. "I'd rather taste it on your lips."

Eleanor set her teacup on the desk. "Who am I to deny you anything" She wanted him to kiss her. There was nothing she craved more. He didn't wait for another invitation. George pulled her into his arms and kissed her senseless, that is, if she had any sense to begin with. Otherwise, she would never have agreed to a whirlwind courtship and wedding.

Six

Eleanor had never considered what her wedding, if she were ever to marry, might be like. Dreaming of her potential future husband had not been something she had thought to consider, so therefore, her wedding day hadn't been high in her imaginings. If she had fantasized about any of it she would now be surprised at the groom fate had in store for her. The Duke of Cranbrook was any lady's dream of a husband. He was kind, handsome, and scandalously attentive.

The wedding itself had been a blur. She could barely recall saying any vows. If anyone were to ask her if she had a favorite moment, she would be hard pressed to name one. No mere moment from that day was worth compounding on. For her, the fact that she was now the Duchess of Cranbrook was the most important facet. Not because she was a duchess, but because he was her husband. The title was incidental compared to the man.

"Do ye have any regrets?" the Duke of Allister asked her. Eleanor's husband, and she still couldn't believe that part was true, stood several feet away from her. He was discussing something with the preacher who had married them. She wasn't certain what, but then again, she didn't care.

"Why would I have regrets?" she asked Allister. George was everything to her. How that could have happened so fast, in so little time, she couldn't imagine. But it was true nonetheless.

He shrugged. "I don't suppose it would matter if ye did. Undoing a wedding is more difficult than planning one. Once the vows are spoken, the two participants are well and truly stuck."

She wrinkled her nose. "How unromantic."

"I'm a realist, love." He sipped from his glass. The amber liquid inside glowed in the candlelight. "Romance is for the foolish. I have no intention of ever being so besotted."

Eleanor wasn't sure how to respond to that. He must be quite lonely with an outlook so contemptu-ous. "I'm sorry you feel that way." She wished she could do something to change his mind. He'd done her a kindness in hosting them for their wedding. If she could find a way for him to find happiness, she would do so. Everyone deserved to find a spot of joy in his or her life. "Why do you feel so strongly against love?" It wasn't romance that he objected to. Something told her that he could be romantic if he wished to be, but love would frighten any cynic.

"I've seen the damage love can do," he told her. "It's not a risk I'm willing tae take." He tilted his glass as if to salute her. "That doesn't mean I wish ye unwell in yer marriage. Quite the opposite in fact. Cranbrook is a friend, and he appears tae be happy with his choice. I hope that remains true for both of ye."

Eleanor frowned. He didn't sound as if he believed they would have a happy life together. "No marriage is without discord from time to time. I don't expect him to be perfect. That would be unre-alistic." She tilted her head to the side. "There is much we don't know about each other. That's part of the adventure. Our journey begins here, and with each day, something new will reveal itself. Our marriage will be anything but boring, and I like to think, that even through the difficulties that might arise we will still have a measure of happiness. Not because love is easy, it's never that, but because we are open to what it can bring us."

She didn't realize until that moment that she did truly love the Duke of Cranbrook. George had sneaked his way in to her heart and burrowed there. "If I were to have one wish, and I like to think on my wedding day I'm allowed one, it would be that you find a way to open your own heart, Your Grace. One day, a woman will find a way into that heart of yours, and I hope you have the good sense to recognize the gift for what it is."

He shuddered. "In that I pray ye be wrong," Allister told her. "I do realize I have tae marry one day, but love has no part in that future marriage. I promise ye my heart will not be a factor in that decision."

"I suppose we will have to see what happens," she said in a calm tone. "As you have not met your future bride yet, we won't know until you do. Besides, I doubt fate will give you much choice. It certainly didn't give me one."

"That's one way of viewing yer marriage," Allister told her. "It appears yer husband is ready to claim ye. Enjoy yer wedding night, lass. I hope it is everything ye imagine it will be." With those words, he walked away from her.

Eleanor didn't know what she hoped her wedding night would be. She hadn't allowed herself to think about it much. That would only make her more anxious with each passing moment. She didn't have anyone to discuss it with her, anyway. She had a brief moment earlier in the day when she had considered all of it, but then quickly set it aside. It was better not to dwell on things that would only make her uneasy.

"Hello, Ellie, love," George greeted her. "It's done. There is no undoing any of it now."

"Would you if you could?" She lifted a brow. "The Duke of Allister asked if I have any regrets. Do you?"

He shook his head. "Never." His lips tilted upward into a sensuous smile. "Do you?"

She shook her head. "Regrets are for people that don't know what they want. I want you. There is no room for doubts in my heart."

George grinned. "Good. Because I plan to ensure that you don't ever doubt me or what I feel for you." He took her hand in his. "Come, wife. It's time that we enjoy our wedding night in full."

THE DAY HAD GONE BY FASTER THAN GEORGE COULD HAVE imagined. He had a wife. Ellie was his forever, and in a few moments he planned on stripping her bare and kissing every inch of her delectable skin. He led her to the bedchamber that they had been assigned to and pushed open the door. Candlelight filled the room and glowed around them.

Once they were inside, he pushed the door open and pulled her into his arms. He pressed his lips to hers and tasted her mouth. She moaned as he swirled his tongue against hers. George skimmed her waist with his hand and then slid his fingers upward until they brushed her breasts. He lifted his mouth and then began to trail kisses over her cheek and then down to her neck. "You're so beautiful."

"Kiss me again," she demanded. She sounded almost drunk with passion. He could relate. Desire corded through him and he was strung tight with need. George wanted to bury himself deep inside of her, but he had to go slowly. This was her first time, and he had to make it good for her.

"I will," he told her. "I plan on kissing you everywhere." George spun her around and began to unbutton her gown. When it was loosened, he pushed it down. He removed every inch of her clothing with ease until she stood before him in nothing but her shift. That would go soon too. He kissed her shoulder as he lifted the shift and pulled it over her head. "So bloody beautiful." He stared down at her pert breasts and licked his lips.

George pulled her forward and leaned down to suck one of those pretty pink nipples into his mouth. She moaned as he licked and nipped it, then did the same to the other one. He slid his hand down her waist and then to the apex of her thighs. George glided one finger over her sensitive flesh. She was so wet and hot. He pushed that finger into her tight center. Her moans grew louder with each of his ministrations.

He lifted her into his arms and carried her over to the bed and laid her on it. Then he stepped back and began to remove his clothes. Once he was fully undressed, he returned to her. It would be so easy to push himself into her welcome heat, but she still wasn't ready yet. Not completely anyway.

"I've never seen anything more beautiful than you." He had never wanted a woman as much as he did his wife. "I need you so much."

"I need you to." She patted the bed. "Come, join me."

George didn't need another invitation. Instead of crawling onto the bed and taking her though, he walked over and stood above her. "I'm not done kissing you yet." He raked his gaze over her flushed body. "I intend to taste every inch of you, love. You've beguiled me and I intend to return the favor."

He didn't bother to explain his intentions. George pushed her thighs apart and pulled her to the edge of the bed, then he settled his mouth at her core. With one lick, she shouted out his name and squirmed underneath him. He wouldn't let her escape. Her pleasure was his ultimate goal, and giving it to her would bring some back to him. He brought the sensitive nub into his mouth and he sucked. Her moans grew louder and louder. She was close. George slid a finger into her and nipped on her clit, then soothed it with his tongue as he pushed another finger inside of her.

She exploded and groaned out her pleasure. "George…." Her body relaxed against the bed as her climax receded. "That was…"

"Exquisite," he supplied the word for her. "You are all lovely and pink." He didn't join her on the bed. Instead, he lifted her legs and wrapped his arms around them, then he positioned his cock at her entrance. "And soon you be mine. Only mine." He pushed himself inside of her and barely held back a groan.

"That's..." She writhed underneath him. "More," she demanded. "I need more."

George pushed all the way inside of her. She froze for a moment as he breached her maidenhead. He waited for her to fully adjust to his invasion. When she started to move against him, that was the only sign he needed. She was ready for more. "You feel so good, love." He slid out of her and then back in. With each stroke, his pleasure built until he thought he could never feel anything quite so wonderful again.

She bucked underneath him, and he quickened his pace. There were no more words. Only their desire and need spun around them. Eleanor's climax rippled around him and squeezed his cock. Her screams of pleasure echoed around the room. His own climax was about to explode and he couldn't hold it back anymore.

He didn't want to.

George groaned as his seed spilled out and filled her. He'd never felt anything like that in his entire life. He was no virgin and hadn't been for many years; however, with her it seemed as if it were his first time. Perhaps it was, in a sense. She had been made for him alone, and sex with her was life altering.

He pulled out of her and then lifted her into his arms. George cradled her against him as he nestled them on to the bed. He pulled the covers over them both and kissed her forehead. "You're mine now. I'm never letting you go."

She chuckled lightly. "As if I would ever leave you."

George's heart lurched in his chest. He couldn't imagine a life without this woman. "I love you," he told her.

"I love you too," she replied, then yawned.

He smiled. He'd worn out his wife. A more gentle and kind husband would allow her to sleep, and he would, in time. He wanted her again, though, and he intended to have her. George would have her as much as she allowed before the night was over. He leaned down and pressed his lips to hers and started making love to his wife all over again.

Seven

The carriage came to a stop in front of Cranbrook Castle. They had left early that morning to return home. Waking up and preparing to leave had been difficult after a night of lovemaking, but somehow he'd managed to pry his eyes open. He had helped his new wife bathe and then dress. They had packed little for their overnight stay in Scotland, so preparing to leave hadn't taken that long. Once they were on the road, he contemplated having his wife again in the carriage but decided against it. She was probably sore from all the attention he'd given her the night before.

"Are you nervous?" he asked her.

She stared out the carriage window at the castle

and nibbled on her bottom lip. "A little," she admitted. "Yesterday I was a mere governess."

"And now you're my duchess," he told her. "The staff will treat you well. I promise." He'd sack them all if they did anything less.

"It's not the staff that concerns me." She blew out a breath. "Your nephew and the countess might not look upon me favorably. I have climbed well above my station by marrying you."

He probably should be concerned about that, but he couldn't muster the necessary feelings regarding it. He'd done as he wished and everyone else be damned. The only person he was truly concerned about was Eleanor. "I left a note for my sister. She will be expecting me to return with you as my wife. Trust me, she will not be difficult. Lady Craven never acts out of place." Besides, it wasn't his sister that actually concerned him. If Lady Felicity Abbot hadn't departed, she would make a fuss. The lady didn't understand the meaning of propriety.

George stepped out of the carriage and assisted his wife down. They strolled into the castle together. No one was there awaiting them and he was glad for it. The servants were all acquainted with Eleanor. He'd speak with his housekeeper and butler and inform them of her change in status. The duchess's bedchamber would need to be aired out and prepared for her.

They hadn't gotten far into the foyer when they were greeted by the butler. "Pardon me, Your Grace," he said, then bowed. "I was delayed in arriving."

"It's all right," he told him. "We are not in need of assistance. But since you're here..." He glanced down at his wife. "There are some things I require done immediately."

"Yes, Your Grace," he said. "What do you require?"

"I've married," he told him. "The duchess's rooms need to be cleaned and prepared, and all of Her Grace's belongings need to be moved. I trust you will see it done."

"Of course," the butler told him. "I'll speak with Mrs. Hopson and make the arrangements." With those words, the butler spun around and walked away from them.

Voices echoed in the distance, and George had a bad feeling. It wasn't just his sister he heard. Which meant that Lady Felicity Abbot still remained. They were in the sitting room. He sighed. "We should speak with my sister," he told Eleanor. "Then you can rest from our journey. Your room will take time to be prepared. If you wish, you may rest in my bedchamber until then." He grinned. "I'd prefer that you do, actually. We can rest together."

Her lips twitched. "Somehow, I don't think resting is what you have in mind."

George wiggled his eyebrows at her. "You know me so well already. I do wish to rest, but you're right." He tilted his head to the side. "There are many, many things I wish to do that have nothing to do with sleep." He lifted her hand and placed it in the crook of his arm. "Come," he said with resignation. "Let's speak with my sister, and then we can retire for a few hours away from prying eyes."

They walked into the sitting room. He'd been correct. Lady Felicity Abbot had indeed remained. Her greedy gaze raked over him, then Eleanor. Displeasure filled her face as her gaze settled over his arm looped with hers. "Sorry I'm delayed," he told his sister. "I trust you received my note?"

"I did," Lady Craven said. She smiled at Eleanor. "I understand congratulations are in order. I must admit I was surprised by your news. Was there a reason you were rushed to Scotland?"

"Only by my desire to have what I wanted most," George told her. He turned toward Lady Felicity Abbot. "May I introduce my wife, the Duchess of Cranbrook."

Her face soured. "Your Grace," she greeted. "It's a pleasure to make your acquaintance."

George prayed that the woman would depart soon. Now that she realized she could never force him into a marriage, he didn't want. He had the woman he desired most at his side. Perhaps it was reckless to rush into a wedding, but having that scheming woman under his roof had made him act rashly. He didn't regret his decision, though. Eleanor was his wife, and that was all that mattered to him. "If you'll pardon us. We only just returned from our journey. We're going to rest until the evening meal. We will join you then."

"Yes," Eleanor said. "We are quite tired."

He barely held back a laugh at her words. George was nowhere near tired... George led Eleanor out of the sitting room. He didn't want her near Lady Felicity Abbot longer than necessary. Something told him that the lady wouldn't leave until she had her say. He didn't understand the woman. Why did she insist on trying for something that would never happen? He only hoped that she left his wife alone.

They reached his bedchamber, and he opened the door. Eleanor walked inside and he followed behind her. He closed the door and clicked the lock into place. George didn't want anyone to disturb them. He planned on spending the rest of the after-noon with her in his arms, and maybe they would be both too tired to join his sister for dinner...

ELEANOR FINISHED PLAITING HER HAIR AND WINDING IT UP into a simple chignon. Her new husband had tried to convince her to remain in bed with him. They could have a tray brought up for dinner, but she refused. That was not how she wanted the servants to view her on her first day as the duchess at Cranbrook Castle. She had been the governess the day before. If she stayed in bed and ate her dinner there with her new husband, what would they think about her? She wanted their respect, or at least something resembling that.

"Are you sure I can't coax you back to bed?" George asked.

"Yes," she told him, and then smiled. "We can return to your bed tonight. You're insatiable."

"Only with you," he told her. He sighed and then kissed her cheek. "I'll escort you down." He'd been ready for a quarter hour and had been waiting for her to finish her hair. He insisted she needed a maid, but she had none. They would have to hire her a lady's maid. One that understood what a duchess required, especially since Eleanor didn't have any experience with such things...

She stood and looped her arm through his. They exited the bedchamber and descended the stairs. Once they reached the bottom, they walked into the sitting room. The Countess of Craven and her guest were already there. "Finally," Lady Craven said. "We were beginning to think you were not going to join us."

"I considered it," George admitted, then grinned. "But I told you we would be at dinner and here we are. Shall we go into the dining room?"

They stood and exited the sitting room. Dinner was served. Once they were finished with all five courses, the ladies excused themselves and went to the sitting room. Eleanor felt ill at ease. She did have some manners to fall back on. She had been a vicar's daughter and had attended many meals with the aristocracy, but she'd never been the highest ranking lady at one.

They all sat, and she stared at a candle on the wall. She had nothing to add to their conversation. Would George be joining them? When could she excuse herself and return to their bedchamber. Her room had been finished hours ago, but she hadn't wanted to leave him and still didn't. She liked sharing his bed.

"I'm surprised," Lady Felicity said.

"At what?" Lady Craven asked.

"That the duke has finally taken a wife. Many didn't believe he would unless someone forced his hand." Eleanor met the lady's gaze. What was she implying? "Did you trap him?"

That was awfully bold of her. "Not that it is any concern of yours," Eleanor began. "But we married because we love each other. I would never have forced him or any man to marry me."

"But were you not the governess?" She sneered. "You're the last woman society would have expected him to make his duchess."

Lady Craven frowned. "That's enough," she said in a firm tone. "You may not approve of my brother's choice, but I do. If you are unable to be gracious, then perhaps you should cut your visit short."

"My apologies," Lady Felicity said. "I'm only trying to understand how this marriage came to happen." She met Eleanor's gaze. "After all last I spoke to the duke, he told me that he would never marry."

"That's not quite true," George said from the entrance to the sitting room. "I said that you were the last lady I'd ever consider taking as my wife. Especially after you tried to trap me into such a union. Why are you actually here, Lady Felicity?"

Lady Craven glared at her guest. "You didn't mention that to me when you wrote and requested to visit." Then she turned to her brother. "I wish you had said something. I would not have encouraged her to travel here."

He shrugged. "I didn't think it would be something we would or should have to discuss. I made my intentions clear." He glanced at Eleanor and smiled softly. "Besides. I met the woman I wished to make my wife when I returned home. I couldn't be happier."

Eleanor returned his smile. She couldn't be happier to be his wife. Warmth spread through her and she nearly melted with the love that overpowered her. How had she gotten so lucky as to have won this man's love? She turned back to Lady Felicity. "Perhaps you should cut your visit short. It appears your reason for traveling to Cranbrook Castle was not the one you presented to Lady Craven. You're no longer welcome here."

"That's not your decision to make," Lady Felicity said and lifted her chin defiantly. "I'm not your guest."

Eleanor lifted a brow. "And this is my home. I am the Duchess of Cranbrook, and if I no longer wish you to remain, then you *will* leave." She narrowed her gaze. "I won't have a woman in residence that makes my husband uncomfortable. Clearly, you have outstayed the little welcome you had. Do not make things more difficult than they need to be."

"You're quite rude," Lady Felicity said.

Lady Craven laughed. "And you do not understand the meaning of the word. You've been discourteous since my brother returned home and you realized he was married. My new sister is right. You are no longer welcome here."

Lady Felicity stood and stormed out of the room. Good riddance, as far as Eleanor was concerned. She hadn't left soon enough in her estimation.

"My apologies," Lady Craven said. "I wouldn't have invited her to visit if I'd known..."

"Think nothing of it," George told his sister. "I should have explained it to you yesterday, but I had other matters I wanted to accomplish." His gaze met Eleanor's. "I have no regrets."

"I'm glad you're happy," Lady Craven said. Then she turned to Eleanor. "And I'm glad he found it with you. I'd like to officially welcome you to the family."

Eleanor beamed. "There is no place I'd rather be."

She loved her husband. They may have had a whirlwind courtship, if one could consider their beginning that, but their love was real. She had no doubt it would stand the test of time. They had a lot to learn about each other, and they would spend the rest of their lives unraveling each other's secrets. Eleanor couldn't wait to start.

He leaned down and pressed his lips to hers, then whispered in her ear. "I love you," he said.

She closed her eyes and let those words wash over her. "I love you," she told him.

Everything would be all right. She believed that to the very depths of her soul. He was her duke and hers alone. This was where she belonged.

Epilogue

Over twenty years later...

Eleanor sat in the sitting room at her son's, Daniel, the Marquess of Hollibrook's etate. She had been married to the love of her life for several years now. That love had given her a son she cherished, and now she would have a new grandchild to give some of that love to. Daniel's wife, Amelia, was about to give birth to their third child. They already had two children, Everett, the Earl of Brookfield, and Genevieve.

"You're anxious, love," her husband said. "Amelia will come through it fine. Just as she had the other two times."

Eleanor had never became pregnant again. They

had tried often, but Daniel was her only child. It was a blessing to have grandchildren. "I'm certain you're right." She could't help her worry though. She hated to imagine what her son might go through if he lost his child or his wife. That was a horror she'd never with upon anyone, espeically her son.

Her husband lifted her hand and pressed a kiss to her palm. "Life is full of surprises. It's how we handle them that define who we are. Whatever happens we will take care of it."

She nodded. Her greatest challenge was learning how to be a duchess. Eleanor would never regret marrying George. Her love for him was everything she could never have imagined. They had only grew to love each other more over the years. "Yes, we will," she agreed.

The door swung open and her son entered the sitting room. A wide grin was on Daniel's face. His dark brown hair was a little disheveled but his gray eyes were alight with happiness. "It's a girl," he told them. "Mother and baby are well. We have named her Gabriella."

Eleanor placed her hand over her chest. Her heart beat heavily inside of her chest. She had worried over nothing. She now had one grandson and two granddaughters. She was blessed. "When can we see her?"

"Soon," Daniel told them. "The doctor will let you know. I'm going back to my wife's side. I jsut wanted to give you both the good news since you've been waiting for hours now."

"Go," George told their son. "We will be all right on our own. Go be with your wife. She needs you more than we do."

"We're truly blessed," Eleanor told her husband.

He leaned over and pressed his lips to hers. "I have never been more sure of anything. Since the first moment I glanced you're way you've beguiled me. I love you, Ellie dear."

She placed her palm on his cheek and then leaned into him. "You have all of me, forever. I love you."

They had lived a good life together. Whatever fate had left for them she welcomed it. Eleanor had no regrets, and never would.

Thank you so much for taking the time to read my book.

Your opinion matters!

Please take a moment to review this book on your favorite review site and share your opinion with fellow readers.

www.authordawnbrower.com

Defying the Duke

WAYWARD DUKE'S ALLIANCE BOOK THREE

ARI THATCHER

Blurb

When her father died, Dinah Westfall was grateful to the owners of Tantalus, a scandal-rich gaming hell, for allowing her to continue to work as their bookkeeper in his place. Her sister and grandmother depend on her income, so she ignores the activities going on around her office. Until a drunken guest assaults her.

Her rescue by co-owner Jack Hill, Duke of Abingdon, comes in the form of a kiss, a powerful, tempting embrace that destroys her sanity. Seriously? He couldn't just punch the man and be done with it? He's a champion of Gentleman Jackson's ring, for goodness sake! Now Jack insists on escorting her everywhere she goes, and his hints at wanting more than a kiss are beginning to tantalize her. She will be no man's mistress, not even a duke's, and will do what it takes to defy his propositions.

Order here: **https://books2read.com/DefyingtheDuke**

Her Duke of Sin

⌘

WICKED WIDOWS' LEAGUE BOOK THREE

Miss Juliet Adams would be living on the streets if not for the kindness of the dowager Countess of Wyndam. Her father died leaving her penniless and without any prospects. The countess offered her a position as her companion and she leapt at the opportunity. She's content with her life, but she's also no fool. She fully realizes a day may come where she won't have the protection of the countess and then where will that leave her...

Gideon Pryce, the Duke of Sinbrough has led a life filled with the most sinful activities imaginable. There's not much he hasn't done or would consider doing. He lives for all the decadence he can indulge in and as far as he is concerned there isn't enough in the world. Until one day he notices her. The one woman that looks at him like he's nothing. Women usually scramble to be with him, but not Miss Juliet Adams. He decides to make it his mission to change her view of him, and perhaps show her how much pleasure he can give her.

Juliet is not prepared for the Duke of Sin himself taking an interest in her. He threatens every carefully laid plan she makes and he might just be her undoing. That is if she can't instead be his salvation...

Order here: https://books2read.com/HerDukeofSin

Excerpt: A Lady Never Tells

LADY BE WICKED BOOK ONE

The first book in an all new series: Lady Be Wicked featuring Eden, The Countess of Moreland from Her Rogue for One Night

Blurb

Eden Barrett, the Countess of Moreland, is a young widow. Her foolish husband died in a duel, after having an affair with her closest friend. With one affair her entire life changed. Having freedom for the first time in her life she embraces it. Roslyn, her sister by marriage, is about to debut and Eden is her chaperone, and she's determined to aid her to find a husband that won't disappoint her.

Maxwell Holden, the Duke of Carrington has decided it is time to find himself a wife. He has a list of requirements and Lady Roslyn Barrett is the perfect candidate. There is only one problem: her chaperone. Something about her is oddly familiar, and he's more drawn to the young widow than he likes. The more time he spends with her, the more he can't stay away.

Eden is determined never to marry again. Especially to the Duke of Carrington. She has a secret though and if he discovers it everything will change. They've met before, and she's determined he never realizes exactly how they're acquainted. Secrets don't stay buried though, and this one is about to come to the light...

Order Here: **https://books2read.com/ALadyNeverTells**

Prologue

Her anxiety had hit an all-new level. Eden Barrett, the Countess of Moreland, did not take risks. It went against her very nature to do so. Yet, that was exactly what she was about to do. She'd willingly accepted an invitation to the Duke of Sinbrough's masquerade ball. It was literally entering into a den of iniquity. Sin itself would be on full display at this ball. The duke was famous for having the most debauched parties for anyone who wished to attend. It was rumored even the most strait-laced ladies would don a mask and join the festivities.

She should be all right. Shouldn't she?

If she kept telling herself that then perhaps, she would be. She'd convinced her good friend, Mrs.

Claudine Grant to attend the masquerade with her. She'd even commissioned scandalous costumes for them both. Eden's gown was the pure white of innocence, but it was anything but that. It was made for sin, and she hoped she would live up to the invitation it presented.

Her mask was also white to match the gown, but it had ruby red feathers fashioned to it on one side. A little splash of color to show she wasn't as innocent as the dress may suggest. Just in case the low-cut bodice didn't do the job. She had left her golden blonde hair loose and flowing down her shoulders. Her mask kept them from going wild, but if it was removed then they might just become unruly.

"Are you ready?" Claudine asked.

"As I'll ever be." She smiled at her. Eden tried to embrace her inner wickedness, but so far it seemed to be hidden. "Someone is about to approach us." She nodded slightly at the direction of two gentlemen making their way through the crowd. "I do believe the gowns are working." She'd had Claudine's gown designed in a decadent pink that nearly matched her friend's skin tone.

Claudine grinned. "One of them is the man I hoped to see tonight. I'd recognize him anywhere."

"How fortunate that he's noticed you as well."

When the two men reached their side Claudine's love interest stared at her briefly before he held out his hand and said, "Dance with me." Claudine went off with him willingly leaving Eden alone with the other gentleman.

"Would you like to take a spin around the floor." The man said.

There was definitely something sinful about him. His hair was as black as his clothing, and his eyes were a very pretty green. She tilted her head to the side and studied him. "You're the Duke of Sin aren't you."

"Was I being too obvious?" He grinned. "Would you like me to live up to that moniker?"

Eden wasn't interested at all in him. He might be sexy as well, sin, but she didn't find him all that interesting. She wanted to feel something. She didn't know exactly what, just that he didn't do anything for her. She shook her head. "No, thank you."

Someone laughed from behind her. "Have you lost your touch old man."

The Duke of Sinbrough frowned. "Don't be ridiculous. That would never happen." He wiggled his eyebrows at Eden as if that said everything. "We're just becoming acquainted."

Eden turned around to glance at the man who had just entered behind her. He didn't wear all black like most of the men in the room. However he had not bothered to wear a waistcoat and jacket. He had on dark blue pantaloons and a stark white shirt, but no cravat. He had left his shirt open giving her a nice view his neck, and part of his chest. The gentleman was completely disheveled. His hair wasn't nearly as dark as the Duke of Sinbrough's. It was more brown than black, but his eyes were a similar shade of green. Where she had found the duke's pretty, this man's were filled with heat.

That heat spread over her like a whirlwind. She'd been looking for someone to spark something in her. Eden had started to believe that she couldn't feel true passion. What was it about this man that made her want more? Was this desire? How had she never felt anything like it before. She took a step toward him and tilted her lips upward into what she hoped was a wanton smile. "Do you think you can do better?"

He returned her smile and it sent shivers right through her. "I know I can," he told her. "Would you like me to try?"

"You mean you haven't already?" She tilted her

head to the side. "Wasn't that what you were doing when you slid your way behind us?"

He chuckled softly. "You may be right." He leaned forward and said in a demanding tone. "I want you?"

"Do you?" She licked her lips. "I might let you have me." She stepped closer and trailed her finger over his collarbone. "But the night is still young. I have many options. What makes you my best choice?"

She'd never flirted like this in her entire life. Eden felt alive for the first time. The thrill of this was beyond even her wildest imagination. He stepped closer until her breasts rubbed against his warm chest. Her nipples tightened at the mere hit of his heat and the pleasure was intoxicating. He leaned down until his mouth was near her ear. His breath caressed her skin making her even hotter with need. "Darling," he said in a husky tone. "You already decided. Don't make me beg."

Her throaty chuckle sounded foreign to her ears. Who was this wicked, wanton, widow allowing this unknown gentleman to seduce her? She didn't recognize herself but wasn't that why she'd come to this masquerade. She slid her hand down and pulled out his shirt from his pantaloons, then slid it underneath until her fingers met his naked flesh. She trailed her fingers up his chest and then around his waist. He yanked her closer. "You're playing with fire, love."

"But what a burn it'll be," she replied in a husky tone. "You did say you wish to play with me tonight. Dazzle me with your skills."

"It'll be my pleasure," he said as he lowered his mouth. When his lips touched hers, she forgot everything, even her own name. Yes. This is what she had come to the masquerade for. She hadn't known what she'd been looking for until he'd come near. Damn this was good, and she suspected as the night rolled on she'd experience more passion than she'd ever known in her marriage.

She wanted him, and she'd have him. Then after this night she would go back to the proper Countess of Moreland. She had to keep up appearances after all. There were people that depended on her. But for this one night she could have him and all the pleasure this kiss promised. No one else had to know. A lady never tells her secrets, and this one she would always hold dear.

Order Here: **https://books2read.com/ ALadyNeverTells**

Acknowledgments

For all the authors that are on this journey with me with the Wayward Dukes'. Thank you for taking a leap of faith and writing in this world.

A special thanks to my step sister, Amanda. Without you I might have lost my mind ages ago.

About Dawn Brower

USA TODAY Bestselling author, DAWN BROWER writes both historical and contemporary romance. There are always stories inside her head; she just never thought she could make them come to life. That creativity has finally found an outlet.

Growing up, she was the only girl out of six children. She raised two boys as a single mother; there is never a dull moment in her life. Reading books is her favorite hobby, and she loves all genres.

www.authordawnbrower.com
TikTok: @1DawnBrower

BB bookbub.com/authors/dawn-brower
f   facebook.com/1DawnBrower
🐦 twitter.com/1DawnBrower
📷 instagram.com/1DawnBrower
g   goodreads.com/dawnbrower

Linked Across Time

Saved by My Blackguard

Searching for My Rogue

Seduction of My Rake

Surrendering to My Spy

Spellbound by My Charmer

Stolen by My Knave

Separated from My Love

Scheming with My Duke

Secluded with My Hellion

Secrets of My Beloved

Spying on My Scoundrel

Shocked by My Vixen

Smitten with My Christmas Minx

Vision of Love

Enduring Legacy

The Legacy's Origin

Charming Her Rogue

Ever Beloved

Forever My Earl

Always My Viscount

Infinitely My Marquess

Eternally My Duke

Bluestockings Defying Rogues

When An Earl Turns Wicked

A Lady Hoyden's Secret

One Wicked Kiss

Earl In Trouble

All the Ladies Love Coventry

One Less Scandalous Earl

Confessions of a Hellion

The Vixen in Red

Lady Pear's Duke

Scandal Meets Love

Love Only Me (Amanda Mariel)

Find Me Love (Dawn Brower)

If It's Love (Amanda Mariel)

Odds of Love (Dawn Brower)

Believe In Love (Amanda Mariel)

Chance of Love (Dawn Brower)

Love and Holly (Amanda Mariel)

Love and Mistletoe (Dawn Brower

The Neverhartts

Never Defy a Vixen

Never Disregard a Wallflower

Never Dare a Hellion

Never Deceive a Bluestocking

Never Disrespect a Governess

Never Desire a Duke

CONTEMPORARY

Stand alone:

Deadly Benevolence

Snowflake Kisses

Kindred Lies

Sparkle City

Diamonds Don't Cry

Hooking a Firefly

Novak Springs

Cowgirl Fever

Dirty Proof

Unbridled Pursuit

Sensual Games

Christmas Temptation

Daring Love

Passion and Lies

Desire and Jealousy

Seduction and Betrayal

Begin Again

There You'll Be

Better as a Memory

Won't Let Go

Heart's Intent

One Heart to Give

Unveiled Hearts

Heart of the Moment

Kiss My Heart Goodbye

Heart in Waiting

Heart Lessons

A Heart Redeemed

Kismet Bay

Once Upon a Christmas

New Year Revelation

All Things Valentine

Luck At First Sight

Endless Summer Days

A Witch's Charm

All Out of Gratitude

Christmas Ever After

YOUNG ADULT FANTASY

Broken Curses

The Enchanted Princess

The Bespelled Knight

The Magical Hunt